1 Year 4 Seasons

A nature's truth about life and its creator

Chaitra Katti

Self published

First Printing, 2018

Edition published on Nov 2018 by Chaitra Katti, Bangalore, India

Edition 1, Volume 1

Fiction/Philosophy

This book is a work of fiction and except in the case of historical fact any resemblance to actual persons, living or dead, is purely coincidental

To the energies that surround me
To the energy of wisdom
To the energy of experience
To the energy of knowledge
To the energy of my life and beauty
I express my gratitude to all the spirits and energies,
who made this possible
Thank you
Thank you
Thank you

CONTENTS

Give it a colour;

1 YEAR 4 SEASONS

PROLOGUE

My Master "Only two kinds of people suffer in the world."

I ask "Who?"

She replies, "Bad people and stupid people."

"I know the definition of bad, who is stupid?"

She tells, "The one who believes the world; that life has to be lived in a certain way."

I ask, "So they are stupid?"

She smiles, "Yes, because they are letting those perceptions control their peace."

"Who are bad people then?"

She answers back, "The one who harms himself first and then others."

"How do I know, I am harming myself?"

She, "Awareness." "When someone calls you something bad, watch what you do to yourself."

"There is difference between suffer and struggle. Animals struggle and humans suffer."

I answer, "Animals think life is to be lived;

humans think life is to build a self image. My Master, "To do that, they lose every blessing."

I ask, "What are those blessings."

My Master, "I have called you to," pauses, "to discover everything by yourself."

"I am not in the condition. I am suffering. Help me overcome, help me find a solution"

"Your destiny is already written. No one can change it."

I look at her in disbelief. Life is surrounded by unfortunate events. 'Why life is unfair? People say there is no substitute for hard work. I work hard. I work all day to ensure I have sufficient skills to,' my Master interrupts, "Everybody in this world is controlled by reality. They think that's real. Give up!" she smiles, "Give up."

I am surprised, "Give up, my dreams?"

My Master, "Liberate from success. Don't hold success, free yourself from it. Life becomes fair. You just have one life and you are holding more than one billion thoughts in your mind, for an illusion- success."

I ask, "What is real then?"

She smiles again, "Success"

I get angry, "I don't understand, what you are talking?"

She laughs, "When you hold no thoughts to become happy, you are successful."

I smiled, "That is real?"

She tells, "You can change your destiny, when you know what to hold and what to give up."

I ask, "What to hold?"

She, "Energy"

I ask, "What to give up?"

She gets angry, "I am not here to design your life. It's your duty to do it. I am there to help you."

I, "So how do I know, what these energies are, what is real, what is not? Now I am more confused."

My Master, "Travel, you will get your answers."

I ask, "Which place and where?"

"The world inside you, travel."

"I have done it, but I dint get any solution."

"Okay, start travelling to various countries. Travel wherever you want, which ever place. When you do, pay attention to the smallest details you come across. You will get a message there. Just write those messages in a diary. I will tell you what to do with them."

I nod and she continues, "The spirit will guide you through situations and voices. Listen to your inner voice."

I ask, "I think everyday spirit guides us in the form of situations."

She answers, "Exactly, but we don't make use of

those messages. Anyways, listen to your voices; observe your thoughts and situations around you."

I agreed.

My Master, "Don't come back to me, if you find those answers by yourself. Come back to me after practicing it."

I agreed.

She gives me a white marble stone, "Let this stone take the rays of sun, wind, earth and sky. Just after two days, immerse it in water for an hour. Keep this in your bag. And know that it will protect you."

I agreed, "Bless you"

My Master, "Thank you. Bless you too."

EXPLORED HER INNER WORLD

The search for meaning involves identifying the reason and the purpose. The hunt to understand the essence of life can be achieved when you travel deep within and understand the connection between the thoughts and its reflections in real life.

I let myself, to create this dimension in my universe and called my guide, when I simply chose to travel. In return I understood the harmonious vibrations of universe and the laws of nature.

It was my first trip to Singapore. I had spent last two days in planning the itinerary. Now I am going to nearest mall to buy some clothes for a week's trip. It was Sunday. A flock of people had already gathered near the trial room to try their clothes. I thought, perhaps I can check some more clothes and the crowd could descend in few minutes. But on contrary it increased. This time, I decided to wait in the queue. I stand behind a girl who is about twenty four years old. She had

around ten pairs of clothes in her hand,
I murmured, "I have to wait a long for my turn."

Girls are constantly running from the trail room to its lobby to check themselves up in a larger mirror, placed outside. Nearby is this girl who is closely observing all the clothes, tried by each one of them. Every time she finds clothes of her interest, she leans forward to ask," Excuse me, where did you pick this from," The girls reply 'From section 4' or 'Section 1'

The girl, then quietly notes down in her mind, so that she could go later and pick them up. I have five different tops to try. The girl has like ten different clothes to try. But there was one thing in common, between us; our choices depended on 'how good it looks on someone else.' I now introspect all our journeys and perhaps it's the same, our story depends on the choices that everybody else makes in their life.

Suddenly in the middle of all these, I encounter something. Before, I realise what is happening, I start to walk in the streets of my heart. I walk inside one of my streets: The street named LIFE, filled with shops; shops of all kinds, to live a happy life. I made further investigation on my street called life; everything depended on someone else's choices.

I walk further and I realised that I am free,

free to move anywhere in my world, inside any shop and choose anything I want. But I look around and everybody is fulfilling their mission of choosing their shop based on someone else's opinion. People are at struggle to buy everything and all at once. They are destroying all their happiness, to buy items; they believe will bring them happiness.

I decided to discover every shop of each one of us. The shops that control our self love.

I walked down this street and it let me to dozens of shops. The shops named Ego, Attention, Desires are at first row, guarding me from experiencing other divine shops and their forces. I decided to get into these spaces and understand how these forces affect my street called Life.

I make a stride to discover more about Ego. I enter into this shop and it looks cosy and comfortable. I move further and I sensed a slim pleasant air passing through me. It stimulated me and in a second or so, my ego heals all my scars. I am happy, I decide to relax in this comfortable zone. I sit and suddenly I feel a tremor. I become scared. What is wrong with this beautiful shop? In a minute or so, I feel another tremor. The interiors are being damaged at every tremor. I peeped outside the window. I could see that the disturbance in some other streets are causing tremor in my street called life. And the most vulnerable shop, was the shop I am sitting in.

Each time I witnessed a disturbance in any other street, this shop trembled and damaged itself. It is really risky here, but I don't want to go out, because it has relieved my pain. It has made me feel good. How can I go out? I am battling between fear of losing myself and the pleasure of comfort; I understand this is what an ego does to someone.

I looked around and everyone is experiencing the same. This force is good, it is important, it helped me overcome my pain, but at the same time it does a major damage on a longer stay. Staying here for long is risky. I started struggling and with immense strength I move out, promising that I will stay here, once I am done examining every shop of my street.

I walked to the centre of the street. Some shops have necessary items, some sold artificial items and some other shops have many roads inside. I have to be careful, about which shop I have to move in, because there is an addiction in each shop. Once you head in, it's difficult to move out and this time, I decide to move towards the force, Attention. There are dozens of people here as well. Everybody wants it, but no one knows why.

The huge crowd assures everyone else that the right items are available. I see a long queue lined up to experience, attention. Everyone has a belief; the shop with maximum crowd sells the right items. Each of them is competing to experience attention and no one knows, why. People near the door are fighting fiercely to buy items, they do not need.

I observe that, people have returned from this shop with a wound, yet proud to have experienced the force, attention. Everyone at the queue are at a belief that there is something precious inside, which is why fights have become fierce inside. This makes them anxious. They are scared that they will lose something, which everybody else has. The anxiety is turning to sorrow. People are no more enjoying the queue. They are disappointed at every step in their street called life, only because of one shop: Attention.

Now some more people return from the shop, more wounded, yet proud, because they have not missed on what everybody else is going through. I see around and I noticed something even more interesting, there is a force hidden inside a narrow path. I moved little to know more about this shop. The shop named Self- Awake. I realised that none wants it, because it has least number of people around.

No one knows, much about this shop. No one wants to know, because everybody is busy following the crowd; the wrong shops, which is believed to be right. I stood here and observed that this shop has a road inside. The road that touches soul and mind. The roads are pre-designed for each and every person and it's unique. A guide here ensures that everyone walks their own road. People are very happy here, because they have learnt; there is neither a joy nor a suffering, it's just a belief.

I understood one thing here, the choices you make in real life and choices you make in your shops are same. Based on someone else opinion, you design your happiness. The shops reminded me that there are several choices in my inner world; I have all the freedom to choose what I want and live in that world however I want. Ultimately how we live in our inner world is more important than our outer world.

I immediately smiled and opened my eyes. Now I have only three people ahead of me, and in next twenty minutes, it will be my turn to try my set of new clothes. Again I see the same thing, dozens of girls, trying their new clothes, asking family and friends about their appearance and one nod of theirs, made the girls think that they look good. Now what I noticed in my streets is similar to what I am seeing here: Your existence is defined by how good your life looks to 'them'. You want to have those that society defines it to be 'must have in life' and you are happy when you get them, irrespective of whether that is really necessary in your life. I noted this down in my diary.

I remembered my friend Jerry, telling me about the Psalm. He had once told me "Creator, created each of his beings for a purpose, but we are diverging from that purpose, to chase certain things that are never meant to be ours. We lose ourselves against the purpose we are created and chase all the wrong, that is perceived as right path by others. You are alive because god wanted to create you. He deliberately chose your race, colour of the skin, your talents, your situation, everything was planned. It is not coincidence,"

When you start to feel, your life has no meaning that is exactly the time to remind yourself that you are following the purpose of the world, not the god, because god didn't create you for that. The world has forced you to take part in what they believe to be the purpose of their life.

When an infant is born, he is the purest creation. He knows he could achieve his eternal peace with three most important elements of universe: Food, Shelter and Love. He enjoys every bit of his existence because he knows life is meant that way. He does what he wants to do and fills every moment of his life doing what makes him happy. He uses four powerful emotions: Appreciation, Love, Happiness and Enthusiasm that manifests into an energy and start emitting the frequency required to get what he wants. But, as time passes, man forgets this secret and starts to invent other desires. The desires might not be a necessary element for his survival, but he wants it because he believes world wants it. He chases false desires, created by the world, and starts to destroy his eternal peace.

The baby that is born according to god's choice, starts to accept and behave according to world's choice. This is when the child forgets his purpose and lives according to the purpose set by the world. People who complain about their existence are the ones who are walking the road that was never meant to be theirs."

Suddenly I am nudged by someone, I come to conscious, it's my chance to walk inside the room, and I am surprised; a small shopping experience has so many things to teach. I am very happy, because I have begun to realise, realise the beauty of my world.

I finished my shopping, headed home for dinner. I slept for a while and took off to airport. I am going to the airport after ten long years. I have forgotten the check procedures, exact place of immigration counters and other things. I am little hesitant to ask information to anyone, because if I ask, it looks like I do not know anything. If I look so, I might not be well received by others.

It is almost my first time and any activity for first time is bit insecure. Being first timer in experiencing any early adoptions of the world is assumed as ignorant. A first timer is often perceived as someone who is away from the current happenings. You are late and you have not considered knowing about the important things of the world for long.

Now going to the airport is something, one should have done by the age 25. I stand at the lobby for a while to ask myself "Why the world's opinion on everything, creates a difference in our understanding about who we are? Why is that the world sets perceptions on everything and believes it as right? I am late in adopting everything, but does that mean I am stupid; because I am not doing what everybody is supposed to do at that time? How and why?

I think and I tell myself 'It is not important' and so I go inside. I go inside the immigration counter. The immigration counters are filled with hundreds of people. Now I do not know which queue I have to take. I look for someone's help and I find a girl "Hi are there separate queues for different country." She looks in surprise, but responds, "No there are no such things called countries, all queues are same."

I smile and say "I am flying for the first time with pride," and moved ahead to line up. I now decide to look like a first timer and observe everyone's reactions about my ignorance. In their world I am ignorant and in my world, they are ignorant; far from reality.

The ignorance that everyone has to do certain things at specific time. In one of his speeches, I remember Philosopher Desai speaks about the reality of time

"Time is an imaginary notions humans have set, it is rather a myth. It runs slow or fast depending on the way we measure them." So one's perception of being a first timer even in later stages of life is purely about measuring a superficial element that does not exist.

"A simple truth is that some people do certain things early and some people adopt it late. In creator's dimension, there is no such thing called time; you are designed to perform certain things according to your periodical sphere. This law applies to every bit of our nature. Human always tend to quantify everything,"

"Look at nature," he describes

"Nature is created at its own time sphere, according to its convenience. Look at the seasons; they start at different time in different parts of the world. Summer starts earlier in Asian countries and bit late in European countries. Do lands of Asia, laugh at European lands for experiencing seasons late in the year? Does that mean that lands of Asia are superior because the sun falls on the equator much earlier? Do the trees in Europe vent in anger at the fact that the Asian trees experience the warmth of sun, much earlier?

The nature has its own harmony at its pace and so are human beings. But seldom do we want to accept the pace that is designed by god.

First time is just a matter of time. First time abroad at the age of 50, first job at age 30, first house at age 60, first masters at the age of 40 has its own dimension in the flow of one's life. We try to quantify it with a number: Time. Every person is assigned with his own dimension of time. First house at the age of 20 or 60, doesn't mean you have crossed the perfect time for it. It means it's the perfect time to get it in your dimension of life."

Now it's my first time to fly abroad, luckily not the last. So I boarded the flight.

HIDDEN ANCIENT WISDOM

I am done with my Singapore trip! I made a note of certain things in my diary. I tried hard to understand every situation, but I was not successful.

I come back and my friend, Zoober and I spend three hours, contemplating the river. I tell him my stories and he repeats, "Certain experiences keep chasing us, until we understand the deeper meaning behind it."

He cooks our last breakfast in the guest house and we drive back. We decide to stop in a small village at the periphery of Bangalore. Zoober climbs a steep road to see what is ahead of him. I follow. We see a small, beautiful farm house. Zoober, "Let's explore this place." We move in and to our surprise, we learn that we can lodge there for four thousand rupees and with bold letters it's engraved on the wall 'Escape into serenity.' We decide to stay for a night.

Few minutes later, the farm owner arrives, "Hi Sir, we will serve you the lunch around 1 p.m, till then, let me take you around the farmhouse." We begin to walk. The farmhouse is a five acre land, exactly representing the vast space of human mind. The vastness has given rise to many trees; each of them grown according to their fertility.

"Everything that grows, depend upon the type of your environment and your fruits completely depend on the type of seed being sowed, deep down the truth of your land." He says

For me, trees are the ideal example of our thoughts. Our entire life depends upon the type of seed sowed and its environment. As we walked, I felt this relevance, at the sight of a Mango tree. The Mango tree which had grown according to its own accord, has given rise to many tasty Mango fruits. The owner, "It takes around six long years of hard work to get first round of Mangoes."

"What I started as a seed, grew to a big tree, and now have begun to develop something fruitful," said the owner pointing at a Jackfruit tree, "This took around five long years to bear its first fruit"

The owner continued, "We all grow to certain height and bear certain fruit; everything depends on, which seed you sow in you and how well you nourish them. And if you want any good fruit, please expect it after four years of your constant hard work." "Look at these weeds," he points at some weeds grown between trees, "these take very less time." He said with a witty laughter,

"So you see, if you don't want to wait long enough, you can take these weeds home."

He continued, facing towards Guava tree, "Your mind also needs nourishment. When you sow the seed of positivity, it grows according to that accord and bears good fruit."

We nod with a smile and he gets excited, "Whoever comes here, I give them a small exercise," with a very polite tone "would you be interested?" We said, "Yes",

"Ok, let's go near Tulsi Plantation." We walked for hundred meters and we see a small Tulsi Plantation. There is a big rock beside the plantation. This place is slighting elevated from rest of the land. We climbed the rock to reach the plantation. We can see the entire farm from this place. There are concrete seating arrangements between every array of plants. A small stream passes at a periphery of the plantation and at the end of the arrays, is a small road that connects to all roads.

Now the fragrance of Tulsi, is taking me to trance. He makes us sit near a big square shaped pot. The pot has a very big Tulsi plant in it. The pot is painted in different colours. It has an intrinsic Indian design; almost resembling a temple. At the middle of this huge squared pot, is a small shelf, which is present at each side of the pot. Each shelf has an Indian god, bestowing specific blessing. The shelf that is facing east, has occupied itself with Lord of Wisdom: Ganesha. The shelf in the West has Lord of Wealth: Lakshmi. The shelf facing south has retained Lord of Courage and Strength- Hanuman and the shelf in the north has Saraswathi: Lord of Knowledge.

When the ancient Hinduism took its initial steps on earth, it was mostly associated with welcoming the positive energy and forces. These energies are wisdom, knowledge, strength and so on. But when it became difficult to feel and imagine these energies, different forms of them were created. Those forms were called gods and goddess, which we pray to. Therefore, when we pray to these gods and goddess, we imagine energy of each lord, bestowing on us, in the form of blessing.

The smell of Tulsi is taking me out of my basic human tendency and transforming my mind to universal peace. Owner, "Look at all the trees and plants you came across today. We saw the Mango trees, the Jackfruit trees and think of all the trees and plants we touched and ate from. He continued, "Just like our dreams, each of these plants, took nearly five years to reap the first set of fruits." He paused for half a second and continues, "I sow seeds and I get the fruit I want, because I know from a Mango seed rises only a Mango Tree. I also nourish each sapling with the fertilizers and never let a single weed or any insect to destroy them. Human mind also follows the same process.

When you sow the seeds of optimism it manifests into a positive energy that surrounds your life. You definitely get what you want, all lies in your own thoughts. If your thoughts are filled with perfect pessimism, then the energy around you manifests itself to pessimism. You start to emit a frequency to universe that in turn gives you, what you cultivate inside your mind."

He smiles, "Now close your eyes," we closed, "I will teach you how to cultivate," we said, "Go ahead." Owner, "Now, gently move your focus towards your fist. Let the right fist hold your positive thoughts and left fist hold your negative thoughts." We closed our palm. "Now put all the focus on your thoughts back. Start observing them. When a positive thought reflects your conscious mind, just open one finger from the right fist and do the same with left fist for negative thought."

We started doing as he said. I closed my eyes and started observing my thoughts. For first twenty seconds I was blank, then the thoughts started moving in, like the glucose that moves into blood from the digested rice in our body.

My first thought, "How will I make up my failed career?" I started feeling a sense of fear and immediately opened my little finger from my left hand. I close my eyes and observe my thoughts again, this time it was to do with the baseless accusation; I recently received from my relative. I opened my ring finger from the left hand. Now I realise only two fingers are open from left fist and not a single from right hand, I force myself to think something positive.

The owner nudged my hand, "Don't force, I can see the frown on your forehead, just let it flow, then we will judge." I smiled and closed my eyes. This time it was again the fear of future that really didn't exist. Fear of losing my job, fear of Zoober's job, fear of death of loved ones, fear of broken relationship, fear of financial crunch and so on. When I opened my eyes, all my fingers of my left hand had opened.

The owner continues holding my palm, "When you are sowing these kinds of seeds, why do we always blame god for not doing good things to us, your mind gets what it receives."I smiled. He continued, "Secret of life lies in your own thoughts."

"Practice this exercise every day. For next one week, just count your thoughts with your fingers.

Never force to think positive. A week later, slowly move your thoughts in a positive direction like, think of the things you want in life. Think of the good things that happened to you." He tells, "Remember, whatever you cultivate it takes four long years to reap." I thanked him. A sense of oneness started running through my flesh. I learnt something important. I noted down in my diary

"Let's go for lunch." I said "okay,"

We walked to the main door of the kitchen area. The staffs of the farm house were waiting for us. We sit in front of the owner and waited for our food to be served on the table. Zoober asked, "How many customers you get in a day?"Owner, "Very rare, I get customers." He continued with laughter, "I recently received a call from a person who asked, 'What are the leisure activities in the farm?' I said there is nothing to do. He never turned up."

"We humans never know the pleasure behind DOING NOTHING. We apply for leaves to be involved in busy tourist packages. Everyone wants to be preoccupied with some thoughts or some schedules, even in their leisure time. I have seen these tourist packages of five nights or six days, oh god they churn your body and soul. You wake up early in the morning, skip your favourite meals and roam whole day in the streets, just because you want to make the best use of the package.

I have seen some women falling sick, drinking the ORS and continue commuting in the cab. If people love being so busy, then why do they take leave and then become busy with another schedule which they call as holiday time."

Zoober, "Yes people have forgotten the concept of holidays. Its time to rest your body and soul". He laughs "I dont know, when do they relax their body and mind amidst these hectic tourist packages? They are constantly involved in worrying about; cab driver cheating them, finding a good room, searching the eating spots. It is rather like, working as facility managers in companies."

The owner agreed, "Vacations are meant to be slow and relaxed" sips water and continues, "People nowadays are hesitant to do nothing, even in their vacations. They are at the risk of being mocked by others when they have to answer 'We did nothing.' for the question 'What did you do going there, this vacation?' So we live a life to please others even during vacation. Everything is obligated in life, including vacation. If you are not occupied in busy schedules, skip your favourite routines, your vacation looks meaningless."

"Most of the tourist packages are filled with

schedules that ensures you to skip at least a day's sleep, involve you in hectic schedule of commuting around five different tourist places in a day, force you to cut down your daily meal routine and then if we fulfil these goals, we are delighted that our vacation is successful," He concluded, "at least, you know the fun behind do nothing in a new place."

We laughed at the artificial idea of vacation and relished our meals together.

The following morning we woke up at my own leisure time, nurtured my OCD by having food on time, went for an unplanned walk, had a clueless day and we discovered the peace behind doing nothing in a new place. We walked wherever our mind wandered and enjoyed the freedom of letting our mind wander.

DAY 1- DIVINE UNIVERSE, STARTS TO FAVOUR- CODE FROM SEASON

I arrived at Vilnius Airport on March 5. The city is covered in snow. I knock the gate and the security guard opens it. I smile at him and he frowns at me. I say hello and I get no response. I walk across a small yard and up to a house that my master had indicated. I go in and I see an elderly shaman.

I say, "My master insisted me to stay here."

The shaman, "I know everything." I ask, "Where can I stay?"

She, "You are bound to receive the sun rays towards south of your room. So follow me." She shows me my room and the window is placed exactly at south.

"Where are you going to work for your survival?"

I tell, "I will be doing a business consulting for a company."

She, "How long?"

I reply, "For three months."

She gives me a key, which has a symbol of a pagan.

I ask, "Are you a pagan?"

She replies, "The whole world is pagan, because every day they are touched by nature." She, "I think, we spoke a lot, it's time to go."

She leaves.

I get ready and walk to my new workplace. I am welcomed by my colleagues. My boss Vilija discusses about the project and its deadlines. I worked till 5 p.m. and walk back home. On my way, I stop at a restaurant for dinner. "Can you get me some pizzas?" The waiter in a rude tone "Everything is expensive here, you can go to other restaurant." I am discouraged. I go out.

A week pass and the days are no longer looking comfortable. I am socially isolated and most people are keeping me at distance, because of my race and appearance. My confidence begins to deteriorate; people are mocking at my clothes, my accent and eating habits.

Few more days pass; my mornings started with a mere bread and jam, because that was the maximum I could afford for. I was then being involved in certain tasks that least satisfied my career interest and my days ended at 7 pm. I have no one to talk to, I am distanced in public places and the monotonous routine traps all my enthusiasm.

Ever since, I had read in one of the philosophical books that suggested 'When each day looks the same as the other day, remember you have wasted one of the days.' I had always made sure that each day looks slightly different from the previous day. But this monotonous routine have killed such beliefs, taken away all my enthusiasm and deteriorated my confidence. Whenever, I tried initiating conversation with anyone, I was either disapproved or ignored. I now feel left out.

I decide to book my tickets back home. My master appears all of a sudden "You have to observe the smallest details that you come across. You haven't been doing what is given to you. Next seven days, will be an important period to create or break your destiny. It's a prime time, make use of it. Describe everything you come across in your diary. Be it weather, trees, people's clothes, snow, rain, everything and anything your eyes see." I read this message and somehow I got motivated.

Next morning, I wake up at 7 a.m, wear a solid blue and white shirt with a printed trouser and headed to work. I take a turn towards a bus station at Vivulskio Street. I am walking at a pace of one kilometre per hour. This means I am too slow. This means I am putting all my dedication to observe the smallest details that lay ahead of me.

As I walk, I notice, beautiful white snowflakes, covering the pavements, on either sides of the road. The beauty is stretching beyond my vision. At this point, I experience a beauty that lies in all of us, in one form or the other, which is beyond our comprehension.

I walk further and notice that every tree, every leaf, every bit of nature is covered by snow, reminding me that no one can escape the severity. The leaves are no longer the part of the trees. They all have perished. I move further and I feel the pain of every tree, for their loss of leaves and flowers. 'Oh god, if these trees could talk, they might have reprimanded the terrible cold.' Despite all these, I see only one tree, who is smiling gracefully at this harsh weather. The tree has all the leaves and not a single leaf have turned pale. I walked further to examine the tree. It is none other than the Pine tree.

My voice, "How come you are so green in this harsh winter. You look beautiful and charming amidst this terrible weather,"

The tree replied, "Have you seen how I have structured my body? Can you see how I have tapered my branches downward?"

I ask, "But why"

The tree, "So that I can slide away the snow from me. It will become difficult for the snow to remain on me. That's why the snow neither blocks the sunlight nor affects me. My wide branches allow winds to sweep right through me. My needle shaped thin leaves are waxy and protect me from extreme cold and water loss. It allows me to gather sunlight that is required for my evergreen leaves.

My dear friend, I have bowed down in front of nature's highest power. My body bows and surrenders itself to anything and everything, nature offers. I am flexible to accept nature's supreme with least audacity and that makes me evergreen, lush and beautiful."The tree continues, "I go with the flow. You cannot change things that are beyond your control, but you can alter yourself from how it affects you.

Look at other trees around you; they have lost their charm, because they cannot accept winters. Their branches are standing vertically up, with ego and audacity to fight against the universal laws. They are in pain. You cannot change what is given to you and your happiness should not depend on them."

I sense a light of energy passing through me now. I feel good about all the times; I had lost my job, I was abused of, I was betrayed and mocked at. These were winters; I could have escaped all these by just restructuring my emotions. I closed my eyes and a divine force is leading me inside, deep inside. The forces are changing the shapes and colours of my soul. A new thought is born again, I opened my eyes.

I smiled at this wonderful message and headed to office: *You cannot change what is given, but your flexibility towards them can change your life.*

DAY 2- SHE HEARS A VOICE FROM A HAPPY WORLD

I walked towards the heart of the old town, on a Sunday morning. The narrow streets are packed with people of all ages. The street music is being played at distance.

As I walk along, I see many restaurants filled with people, excited to satisfy their tongue with delicious food. At every hundred metre, there is a vendor, selling his items, for day's bread. The most common items were flowers and paintings. Just when I was admiring the beauty of this old town, my attention gets drawn to an old man who is busy painting his thoughts on a canvas board.

I cross the road, to see the paintings. There are more than one hundred paintings hung on a tree. The paintings are in different sizes, each conveying unique message. I now see that the old man is paying least attention to his customers. He is least concerned about his daily bread; he could earn by attracting the customers, with his manipulative gestures. He is just stocking up his inventory with several art works.

I am little hesitant to ask him, yet I take this

risk and leaned forward to ask "Why do you waste time, working on so many art works, when many of them are yet to be sold? You could instead welcome the customers and pay attention to selling them right now." I knew this could be offensive. I am giving advice on what to do, when he knows what he needs.

The old man instead smiled and said "Love and its feel, cannot be exchanged for money."

"What matters the most for me is doing what I love. If I set a monetary value to this experience, then the infinite spirit in it loses its charm. Life is all about pleasant feel. Money cannot give you that feel, but every touch of my painting does. It changes the whole essence of my life. I can taste every spoon of my spirit, while doing, what I love. But can you feel the same with money?"

He smiles pointing at the art work "I derive a special feeling from these art works. It conquers any kind of monetary compensation.

I have never experienced any feeling with money. It is a mere paper that can only be exchanged, to get what you want, but you can never feel that paper. When I have the ability to feel the touch of infinite in me, why should I bother to get money for it? If you cannot find love within you, you start to search for it. The easiest one to get is money.

Money is deceptive; it tempts you to get what you like. But when you get it, it makes you to forget what you love. You start becoming slave of it and it starts to rule your life. It forces you to love them and get them constantly, failing which, it threatens to destroy, everything you love. Gradually they tempt you to love those things; they can afford and force you to ignore those things that they cannot be afford.

One of the most dangerous things is that they don't let you to love yourself, without them. Because, they know if you learn that art, you will pay no attention to them.

I already have abundance of love in me, I am taught to find love in everything I have. I am not taught to find love in everything others have, that's why I am not depended on money."

Now an aura of fragrance passes through me. I can sense this fragrance converting into love. I examined every part of my soul and body. It needed love, love deep inside; the love for my skill, for every part of my body, for my thoughts, the love for my anxiety. The fragrance is passing through all of them and each of them can sense a special feel that the money cannot afford.

Slowly the fragrance let my resistance to accept love in me. The love for everything I have and the love for everything I don't have. I feel fresh with the smell of my love. Money could not have replaced this experience of love. I look around and the music is being played at distance 'love is more than enough.'

DAY 3- WITNESSES HER DARK WORLD

It was first week of April. As I walk along the road, I see many house owners, cleaning the snow, accumulated on either sides of their house. The winter has withdrawn people from going outdoors. There is emptiness in each day. The emptiness that creates an echo, of our inner voices.

My inner voice begins to wander in the islands of my heart. It wanders from one island to other and suddenly it stops, in one of them. It examines the silence and from deep within, a voice speaks, "The roads in this island are covered in snow. How often does it snow in your islands?" I said, "More than often." The voice continues, "So how often do you clean them?" I had no answer. But I do feel cold inside, because of them.

The voice continued, "Then you better know all your islands, how they are, when they were formed and what is their condition."

I wanted to ask, 'How should I do it? because I know there are still many others islands of mine accumulated with dense snow.'

It continues, "What do you learn from these people, who are cleaning the roads in front of you?

I answer, "They clean, to free their roads."

The voice, "So don't you think the same thing works with your islands too? The wisdom comes from honouring the meaning behind the smallest details of everyday life."

Now I start to examine every island of mine. They are formed by many layers of emotions. The emotion that was created by situations. I begin to move in, to explore them. I see the damaged islands everywhere and they have caused much damage to other islands as well. Everything caused due to the actions of outer world.

The voice continues, "You cannot control your outer world, but you can control your inner islands, because it's yours. Each day you receive a beautiful message, use them to heal your islands. Look at the nature again; Can you negotiate with them to give you winter or summer?" I said, "No." "But you have learnt to deal with them right?" I nodded.

"Just like these temporary seasons, like every season, the ugliness of pain disappears, when it has to, we cannot avoid it.

Many of your islands get affected during tides. But does that mean you do not rebuild your island?"

I now discover many more islands. I can see many more damages, because of floods and snow in my life. I realise that I have never cleaned them since then.

I see around now. I start seeing my reflection everywhere.

The voices begin to distance, "The snow makes its appearance every year, in some of your islands and disappears when it has to. We cannot avoid something that is not in our control neither can we blame our island for having extreme winter. You are on that land because your body can deal with it. You are born to experience every season and it's up to you to enjoy or worry about your temporary experiences. You can even create a new beautiful island based on those experiences.

Winter disappears when it has to and re-appears when it has to. Nobody can avoid it. Most importantly we have accepted it as a part and parcel of nature."

So what about our miseries?

DAY 4- HER FIRST ENCOUNTER WITH A POWERFUL VISION

I walked the streets of Uzupiz. This small place has a separate constitution and as I walk, I come across a wall which has its constitution engraved in twenty different languages. I go near the wall and start reading,

Everyone has the right to live by the River Vilnele, and the River Vilnele has the right to flow by everyone.

Everyone has the right to hot water, heating in winter and a tiled roof.

Everyone has the right to die, but this is not an obligation.

Everyone has the right to make mistakes.

Everyone has the right to be unique.

Everyone has the right to love.

Everyone has the right not to be loved, but not

necessarily.

Everyone has the right to be undistinguished and unknown.

Everyone has the right to idle.

Everyone has the right to love and take care of the cat.

Everyone has the right to look after the dog until one of them dies.

A dog has the right to be a dog.

A cat is not obliged to love its owner, but must help in time of nee.

Sometimes everyone has the right to be unaware of their duties.

Everyone has the right to be in doubt, but this is not an obligation.

Everyone has the right to be happy.

Everyone has the right to be unhappy.

Everyone has the right to be silent.

Everyone has the right to have faith.

No one has the right to violence.

Everyone has the right to appreciate their unimportance.

No one has the right to have a design on eternity.

Everyone has the right to understand.

Everyone has the right to understand nothing.

Everyone has the right to be of any nationality.

Everyone has the right to celebrate or not celebrate their birthday.

Everyone shall remember their name.

Everyone may share what they possess.

No one can share what they do not possess.

Everyone has the right to have brothers, sisters and parents.

Everyone may be independent.

Everyone is responsible for their freedom.

Everyone has the right to cry.

Everyone has the right to be misunderstood.

No one has the right to make another person guilty.

Everyone has the right to be individual.

Everyone has the right to have no rights.

Everyone has the right to not to be afraid.

Do not defeat.

Do not fight back.

Do not surrender.

Some argue that the last three are mottos, not rights.

DAY 5- SHE ONCE AGAIN CONNECTS TO A SECRET- SEASONS CHANGE

We are finally done with winter for that particular year. It is onset of spring. The leaves are sneaking out eagerly to converse with sun. The lull seems to end for them. They are steadily preparing themselves to push their auxiliary and rise as quickly as possible, by making the best use of sucrose, produced by photosynthesis. They are more focussed to grow, rather than wasting their time, thinking how winter spoiled their happiness, for three long months.

The weather forecast suggests that it will rain for a week and then for next fifteen days it's going to be sunny. This is going to be the perfect capsule for all the floras.

I see the first layer of green, capturing the majesty of my eyes. I feel the sun on my face. The little flowers are touching me, through their scents. At his moment, I admire a miraculous power. There is only one wealth in the real meaning of life; the wealth of six senses. As a human all that is needed, is a simple life, with all the senses working perfectly.

I focus on my senses now. I can feel the touch of the sun, fragrance of flowers. I am amazed at the idea of experiencing this wealth every day. There is a beauty in them, to feel the sphere of nature's love every day. I begin to understand the meaning of true love. Love that exists in every bit of nature. I ask myself 'Why do we search for our true love, only in humans?'

I smile, everything in nature is alive, and now I take closer look at my nature. I feel the sun, the wind and everything, that constantly changes. I know in the passing days, sun transforms his intention and it will be summer. The duty of summer will be perfectly done by this miraculous power, irrespective of people complain or not. Again days will pass, and there will be a cool breeze from the east to show the first glimpse of winter. Then again the monsoon evokes to the call of harmony, followed by summer, all of them showing a circle of duty. The duty that is perfectly done by each season, irrespective of people's choices.

I clearly understand two things here: The first thing, nobody can escape from the duty of miraculous power.

Second one, everything changes according to its flow, the principle called a cycle of changes. The season changes, days change and everything that has life will change and abides to the law of universe- rotation of changes.

DAY 6- SHE EXPLORES HER REAL WORLD

It's Day Six. Time to decide, to go back home. I get up and I sleep. I sleep till mid evening. I am free to take decision. I can drop a mail right now to my manager and leave or I can choose to explore. Explore the paths unknown. It's up to me.

Now, there are voices, talking in my head. The voices that all of us hear, when we are on the verge of any decision. The first voice defends our comfort zone and the second voice talks about guidelines, we are born to follow; the guidelines that tell us, what would happen, if you give up. Those are like, your future will be affected, your family, friends and neighbours would mock at your missed opportunity. You might not get an opportunity back. I will be made to understand that giving up is dishonourable. I will be reminded again and again that I missed a chance to improve myself; I am least capable to do anything in the world. I suffer because I am made to understand that giving up is evil.

On the other hand there is a world inside me; that still loves me and tells me to do everything that makes me comfortable.

I need to consider one. For that I need to know the truth. The truth created by world and the truth created by god. I know there is a big difference between them. I want to know which is right and then this truth can make my decision. I have learnt that the secret of happiness is in the real truth.

I start to introspect deep inside. I am beginning to realise something very important. There are worlds inside all of us. Outer world and inner world.

The outer world sets its atmosphere based on other people and their perceptions. You become what you see in your outer world. You start defining yourself, based on perceptions of outer world, about you. Your life is completely designed by their views. What they think as right, is what you start doing.

The inner world is free and distinct. It's your world. They are independent of world's perceptions about life and you. They always want you to do, what makes you comfortable. They are born with you and die with you. They never give up loving you. It's the love of inner world that always keeps you alive.

The outer world on other hand sets rules for everything. The rules that control your inner worlds. The rules that define happiness. Their only job is to set definitions on 'What is required to become happy, what is not? Now it's up to you whether to give that freedom for them to define and control your inner worlds.

I am understanding that the thoughts that emerge in all of us, are because of the functions of outer worlds. I am recollecting all the thoughts, created by them. Every thought, has changed my behaviour. Is it right that I am giving too much freedom to some other world to destroy my peace? Why is that I always ignore my inner worlds, that loves me a lot?

I want to listen to my inner world. So, I travel inside. As I travel, I begin to find myself. I walk inside and I discover that it has my best. I am knowing the best in me. Out of all the ways of living life, the right one is know your best.

I feel happy that there is so much of good in me. I now start to see lights everywhere. The light is intensifying through glitters. I move inside these glitters and again a divine energy passes through me. I focus on it and observe every part of my consciousness. It has no thoughts from outer or other worlds. I understand that our inner worlds have no thoughts, but only love.

I sit peacefully now to know the truth, in one of my lands and slowly a firm, confident voice speaks. I know it's my voice, "Do you want to know the truth of god? The truth is good decision. What is a good decision? Every decision of your life. Then what is a lie- A lie is a perception set by the world about your decision.

A Decision is a result of a thought that wins against numerous thoughts in a battleground. These thoughts are like soldiers, who fight hard, to prove their love for you. How can something fought for your good, can be bad? All the decisions are good because it favours one of the soldier's love for you. Everything is done for your own good. There is no such thing called wrong decision, every decision is right, because all of them are made with a good intention for your future. The decision taken at that situation, at that time is always right because you love yourself more or you value your love.

The decisions that do not work in your favour, does not mean it's a bad decision. The same decision could have worked in someone else's favour."

Now, I look back at every situation, I examined every decision I had made. All the decisions were right because there was an instrument of love for me in every decision. My career, my boyfriend, my behaviour, my attitude, my failed business, everything was a good decision because I valued my love more. I felt amazing and again energy passes through, the energy of appreciation for my love.

I returned back to my situation now and all the things that happened in last six days. They all have elevated a love in me. They taught me to find myself. Find me, amidst laws of nature.

Nothing is a misery, nor a merry, It's only a law. The Laws that creates experiences for a purpose.

I have emerged from a mystical experience. An experience to understand the language of universe. The language of love, the laws of universe and everything penetrated deep inside me, during my silence. Silence, that was often misunderstood as loneliness. The loneliness, that is created for all of us, to remind about our roads.

Universe talks when you are ready, ready to listen to them. It talks through every smallest element on this planet. It conveys a message- Life is neither a suffering nor a joy- it's only an experience

SHE UNDERSTANDS MEANING OF EVERYONE'S PROBLEM

A new employee joins my team. He introduces himself as Adrian.

I ask, "Where are you from."

He, "Germany"

He asks, "How long are you here."

I reply, "Another week and I am done."

At 1 p.m, Adrian, "Can we go for lunch?"

"Sure, I am coming."

We walk for five hundred meters and enter a restaurant. We sit and order some pasta. All of a sudden Adrian asks me, "Do Indians stink?" I felt strange and offended, "No, not at all, why do you think that way?"

Adrian answers, "Sometime back, I was residing with an Indian roommate and he was stinking miserably."

I laugh, "It's just one person. One person cannot represent a country's smell." He laughs too and I am convinced that I clarified his doubt. Three days pass, Adrian asks again, "Do Indians stink." This time I am bit more offended. How can somebody repeatedly ask such questions, without understanding how offensive can it be? I answer back with a no. I go back home, wash all my clothes, sprayed a strong perfume on them; because I am guaranteed that I stink and he wants me to know about that.

Few more day pass and once more Adrian asks the same question, "Do Indians stink?" This time he is trying to offend. He cannot assume that the entire country stinks, just because of one person.

Following morning, our boss schedules a meeting on Business Research Strategies. We head to conference room at 10 a.m. It is a small room that fits a maximum of five people. We are eight in number. Our boss tells us to squeeze through and assures "We will have a bigger conference room in coming months."

We start our discussion on various research agendas. While were discussing, I sensed a weird smell passing through me. I lifted my head up, sniffed for a second, to know the source of the smell. I could not figure out. Few more minutes pass and the smell began to trouble me. I look around to see the source of this ugliness. I again failed. Some more time pass; I suddenly sense this weird smell from Adrian. I got this smell whenever he opened his mouth to say something. Now should I have to tell them "What makes him think, `other's stink'?" I think for a while and decide "Let him find out on his own. Until then, he keeps assuming that everybody else stinks."

FIRST PRINCIPAL IN LAW OF ATTRACTION-LOVE

I just have one week left and I am cooking with the left over groceries for my meal. I am at the kitchen and I meet Joseph and his wife Laura. I speak to them for a while and we connect. They invite me for Easter at their friend's house. I accept the invitation.

We take a taxi at 11 a.m. On our way Laura, "She is my best friend. Her name is Grace. We are friends, since 1994. You will definitely love her passion and ambition. Her husband is Martin and he is from Kenya. He is a pilot." I ask, "Are they aware that I am coming?"

Immediately, Laura and Joseph, "John was very happy to hear that you are coming as a guest. We told him that you are from India." I smile and I thought, 'He finds happiness in inviting a stranger to his house; he must be a great person.' We enter the house and Martin welcomes us. I remove my shoes and walk to the drawing room, there I find Laura's friend, Grace. I moved forward to give her a shake hand and I notice Grace has no legs. I learnt later that she suffers from a strange disability.

I sit on a dining table questioning myself, 'How can Martin fall in love with a disabled woman? Though I have heard and read enough philosophies about love being independent from material possession, but as a matter of fact it is very difficult to adopt in real life.'

Martin served the food, while we were playing traditional Easter game. Laura introduces Grace, "Chaitra, she is Grace, one of the most talented women I have ever seen," She explains how Grace received education accolades despite her disability. "Her disability has made her body stagnant and she cannot move any of her body parts, including her neck. Grace is constantly working on it to overcome that, so that she can chase her passion."

Laura continues her explanation on how she received double masters, studying the toughest subjects, "She works for Central government in the administrative section. She is one of the influential women in Lithuania."

Joseph, "Martin was able to grow his business in a year's time because of Grace's networking skills."

Grace begins, "I could do all these, because 'I love myself' and the way I am created. My parents taught me this love. You see, I am the member of European Disability And Welfare

Association and every year we come across millions of children, suffering from strange disabilities. I have never seen any child blaming their life for that, as much as their parents do. Parents think that their child cannot have a normal life and worry about their survival. In reality, everybody on this earth will have enough of those, that is required to live a life, "swallowing a gulp of water, Grace continues, " The world thinks that if you have all the body parts adhering to a certain standard, you can achieve whatever you want to. Nobody understands that, it is not a mere body, but the thoughts in you that defines the essence of universal success.

Parents want their children to look normal but they cannot understand that their children are always the blessing, for since birth, these children are aware of their weakness and work with passion to fight against the odds of the world. They are the real warriors, because they have learnt to battle since childhood.

When all other children are still under the notion that life is a fairy tale, these children would have already learnt about the reality of life and prepared themselves to fight the battle that comes along. No matter, what kind of disability the child has, it is well aware of the problem and have learnt to deal with it. Parents never understand that, they never confide in their strength. But in my case, my parents were well aware that the perfect thoughts about life, is more than enough to survive a battle. They confided in me and filled me with love. Today I have more than what I need to have in life."

Joseph continues, "If world believes that the people with a body functioning normally, could help them survive and achieve, then the whole world would have achieved what they wanted to, because they have their body and brain functioning normal."

Laura joined, "Then if that were to be true, people like Stephen Hawking, Hellen Keller and others could have never made recognition for themselves. God gifts everybody with everything that is required to live a good life."

Grace continues, "Just like everyone, we too will have no one to take care of us during our old age. Just like everyone we will have caretakers to take care of us and just like everyone we too will earn money," she continues with laughter, "Unlike everyone we have learnt to love and accept ourselves as we are. We never veil our true personality. We shape our life according to our weakness. We know what we can do, what we cannot, unlike the world, who become aware of this at the end of their lives."

We finished our lunch, had some conversation about Martin country's Kenya. He described how beautiful Kenya is and narrated his childhood stories. We had our evening snacks and headed home.

On my way back, I ask, "Laura, How did Martin fall in love with her?" Laura replies, "Martin loves her. He never considered her outer appearances; he fell in love because he says he has never seen any woman who loves herself so passionately. He believes, when one has abundance of love for them, they can spread among others and he has sensed that in every step of his life."

Joseph joins Laura, "When I asked him too about his love, he said that she has everything that is required to fall in love with. 'We have everything that a love should have,' he had once told me 'The world has even set standards to fall in love, they make a list of things, required to fall in love and people are blind sheep following whatever world thinks as right path. When people don't get true love, they cry all their life, because they have been chasing the world's belief of love.' People think material possessions maximises the quality of their love." with laughter.

Laura continues, "He never judged her with her outer appearance; all that mattered was her inner beauty. When one is not confident about their self identity, they depend on the outer appearance of their spouse to boost a self image for them. There is no factor of love here. But in Martin case it is only true love."

This day I learnt and understood law of attraction. Grace has so much abundance of love in her that she striked the perceptions of impossible set by the world and achieved the accolades only because she loved the way she was created. Since she had abundance of love in her she could attract a person who was filled with the same.

Law of attraction: You attract what you have. In Grace's case she attracted true love towards her.

INTERPRETS THE CODE OF BROKEN STAIRS

We decide to climb a hill, Three Crosses. It is an hour's hike from Central Cathedral near the old town in Vilnius. At the top of the hill, lies a prominent monument, Three Crosses.

We are four in number. We begin to climb the hill to witness the power of Three Crosses. My friends Stanley and Laurynas take the lead. Monika and I follow them. Stanley and Laurynas make their giant strides towards the hill, discussing about the political turbulence in Europe. My response, "Why would somebody discuss the problems of the world, in the middle of the hike." In my master's view, trekking/hiking is meant to solve internal conflicts. It tells you to recognise the rare roads meant for you.

I am little opposed to the idea of trekking in a group. There is always a chance of being a misfit, in the objectives. Every one will have an objective, when they trek. Some trek to check their fitness level, some trek to enjoy the view at the end of the mountain, some trek to accompany their friends and I trek to observe every road, every stone I come across, while I walk. I have learnt to compare trekking with the journey of life. Every path consists of various levels. Some paths are smooth, while some are hard and others are dangerous. We cannot avoid any of these paths to reach our goal. Of all the ways in achieving a goal, the best one is experiencing the journey.

Some people intend to walk their roads faster, with a superficial number in mind. They never think about understanding their roads. They want to reach fast, so that they can achieve another goal. They chase every moment and forget to observe the roads.

"There is a joy associated! There is a merry associated! while we walk." said Monika. I clearly understood what she meant. I reply, "Yes, there is no point in achieving any goal without enjoying its journey." I continue pointing at Stanley and Laurynas, "They are climbing because they know, it is meant to be climbed, but I don't think they understand the reason."

Monika agrees, "How could somebody feel the enthusiasm in their journey, when they do not know, why they are climbing." she continues, "Do people really know about their goal?" I, "Mostly not. Most of the times, the world sets a goal. People are made to understand that they have to reach them, during certain time. Everybody follows, nobody knows why. That's why there is no enthusiasm in the journey." Monika sits on one of the rocks and continues, "You know, I have seen people setting their goals and all of them has to do with material possessions. This is a common goal and people never find any excitement, because the goal is not set by them.

When there is no excitement in the journey towards the goal, then the whole concept of achievement becomes meaningless.

The most vulnerable way is to achieve their goal fast.

You know, I have walked several roads. I am made to comprehend that understanding the road is more important than walking fast. At the end of the day, everybody will reach their goal. You need not remind yourself again and again about it, once your mind knows about your goal, it takes you towards that direction. Then what matters the most is how you enjoy and learn while walking on rough or smooth roads."

"I completely agree by you Monika, you know I had tried telling some of my friends about it. But they always argue that they can walk fast, they still can enjoy the journey and learn the lessons of the road."

Monika "How can they, when the law of universe doesn't let it to. Do you know Pauli's second law of physics: Two objects cannot occupy the same place at the same time. The answer is same.

It is so exciting to step on your first road on the day of your birth. Then you move according to god's directions. You start enjoying every path," she points at a puddle, "The roads will have puddles and you fall, you learn to check the puddles, before you take next step, then you learn to handle steep roads and smooth roads. Everything looks exciting. Then after a while you will reach certain height and you look back to enjoy the magnificent journey you had gone through, you will smile at those obstacles and feel the sense of achievement, because you could cross them.

You then ascend even more higher, you again look back, now all those roads you walked through, looks smaller and narrower from the top. You then become aware that you should not forget all those roads you pass, because you will use same roads another day to descent and climb adjacent goal,"

I interrupt, "This is how the journey of life should be."

Monika, "Right. But this is exactly what is not happening. Everybody is in rush. Everybody walk certain roads, because they are made to understand that it's a right path. People lose motivation. They become tired and frustrated, only because the road is not meant for them. Goal makes no sense, if you do not understand your roads properly. It has its value only if you use them properly."

As though she realised something important, she pauses for a while, "Once people go higher, they forget their previous roads. They again will fail, because they have to use same roads to descend and climb another mountain,"

I interrupt, "It's true, let's part our ways to follow our paths." Monika signs as though she needed some more time to relax in her dimension.

I walked ahead now, as I climb, I observe. The road has big and small rocks acting as temporary obstacles. As and when people crossed this, they learnt the idea of art of balancing.

I move little higher, as I moved, I observed that some stairs are broad and narrowed down immediately in next one step. Everyone around are slipping a bit due to the immediate shift from broad to narrow path. I immediately could connect this with the story of all our lives.

Some stairs were broken and people had to jump over two or more stairs to avoid broken stairs. As I reached the middle of the mountain, I looked back and observed that neither the roads, nor the trees are evenly structured. There is a chaos and a beauty in that mess. Everything on the earth is a chaos.

I observe this chaos and there is a strange sensation growing within me. The closer I am getting to nature, the higher is the sensation. I am feeling every chaos, that the nature experiences. Everything that has life goes through a chaos which transforms itself to wisdom.

I returned to my state of conscious, I am agitated; because I never understood the pleasure of the chaotic world. I attached myself emotionally to everything, in the past and so I died every day. I used emotions to describe those chaos in my life. There was a beauty in them. I am now trying to feel the pleasure of my chaotic world, without attaching any emotions. It's pleasure of knowing the unknown adventure.

The pleasure that is felt in your first orgasm. You experience a fascinating sensation in the chaotic thoughts. You don't understand what is happening, but you feel the pleasure. You let the pleasure take your mind and you totally forget everything. You go deep inside your pleasure and you start feeling them, against the chaos. There are no rules here. You could go deep inside the pleasure and there is no limit. You understand your limitless possibility amidst your chaotic thoughts. You get excited, you come back relaxed. You know, that you were not wrong, you did not harm anyone, but your thoughts have become chaotic only because of the world. You observe, how the world sets all the thoughts inside you. You will then learn to ignore the world and feel the excitement.

I now found myself precisely in that secret dot. I looked around and learnt to find myself in the chaos. Everything is chaos because it is meant that way. All I am feeling is a constant desire to feed my soul with excitement.

I look up and I now notice that, Daniel and Laurynas were there on the top of mountain, waiting for us. I smiled, 'this is what will happen if you are too fast in life.'

I said, "It will take time, if you want to leave, you can."

Daniel, "No we will wait, we have nothing to do after this."

I smile and tell myself, "This is what will happen, when you follow the speed of the world."

NATURE REVEALS A SECRET TO DESTINIES

On June 24, I along with Zoober and his friend Vipul went to Malana village in Himalayas. I followed the same objective. 'Once I tell my mind about my goal, it will be printed deep inside it. I need not remind myself about achieving it. All that matters is what road I take? How beautiful I can make my journey?'

This time luckily all of us had same objective, to examine every road, and rejuvenate ourselves, by pausing our external conversation. We spoke less among ourselves and spoke more to our inner soul and re-connected the journey of Malana with the journey of our life.

Each road we took, gave answers to our problems and also the reason of their presence in our journey. The roads exhibited the pattern similar to that of Three Crosses Hill. The broad and narrower steps constantly changed, as and when we climbed higher.

Vipul and Zoober moved ahead and I followed them. We walked for five hundred meters and Vipul, "Lets part our ways." We agreed. They disappeared and now I am all alone to walk my road.

I step on a partially broken platform and it revealed a symbol of conflict, we go through while balancing on a broken step. Broken things demonstrate patience and at this moment I carefully decide to stand on this broken step to learn to balance. I stepped carefully on a rock, and made sure I don't fall. I watched for a second and then realised that my first fall can teach me better: The Art of Balancing. I stopped my resistance to fall and let my body take its free move. I fell and I got up, I am hurt. I fall again; two, three, four times and finally I learned to accept the broken step as it is and instead learnt to balance on it.

Now, I sense a strong current of fear, going far away from me. The fear of falling from a broken step. The fear looks adventurous, because I have understood another secret- The Art of Balancing. The only way we can transform is by exploring the worst. You first allow pinch of fears to pass through you and after few attempts, you arrive at peace. You are awakened because you have understood one thing- You cannot always focus on fixing broken things, all you can do is explore and balance them.

Now I look down, I am still at the periphery of the mountain. The periphery has broad steps. This made everyone conclude that the journey is going to be easy. I climb further, now I observe that the same set of people are disappointed at the difficultly experienced from broken stairs, in the middle of the valley. Their faces become dull. I climb further more, with the same set of people and now we are near the top of the hill and stairs become broad again. A basket of cheers enter their soul, their faces brighten again. All I observed was the emotions that constantly changed based on the shape of the steps. Again, I reconnected this with the story of all our lives.

I reach the top and I see a little shepherd who is happily living with least demands on himself. He is not harming his soul by demanding a lot from himself; all he does is let his sheep gaze and rejoice the essence of success. Suddenly, a beam of sun rays shines on my eyes. The sun offers a magical grace on me, I understood the shepherd's secret of happiness; make everything out of nothing. Living with perfect blend of natural landscape has given him something, something that the world always struggles to get.

I stride further and now I see Vipul and Zoober enjoying in their dimension. I, "Guys, wait for me. I am coming." Zoober replied, "Yes, we will."

We all walk little more and enjoyed the serenity of natural landscape. The marijuana has occupied all the space in the hearts of people.

They look more natural and the leaves have made them real and natural. We look around and it is an amazing view. To the left side there are glaciers covered mountains, almost touching the clouds. They seem, as though, they know the meaning behind touch; touch of love.

To our south is a small lodge and towards right lies the beautiful Malana village. We book a room in this lodge and the owner accompanies us to show our room. He opens the wooden door and I see a beautiful message engraved on it; 'When in doubt, love.' The message speaks the language of universe. I become happy. We sit at the balcony, smoking marijuana and cherished the beauty, life offers us every day.

*

It's early morning. We have to descend this mountain and climb the mountain opposite to it. We finish our breakfast and take strides to descend Malana village. We walk towards west of this mountain for a kilometre and we see a small bridge, from where we had started our trek. The bridge is at east side. We now decide to walk towards east. We walk in this direction for one hour until we reached the middle of the valley.

We notice two opposite roads intersecting here. We looked down again and the bridge (our destiny) is at east. We again started walking in the east direction. We walked for three kilometres and few minutes later, the bridge disappeared from our vision. We become confused about our direction. Zoober, "This means we do not remember our roads." Yes, the secret lied in not only observing the marvels of the road but also in remembering the roads.

We started looking around for help. A villager nearby comes to our rescue, "This will take you to the river nearby, not the bridge." We are disappointed now, we have walked way too long to know that we are in wrong road.

I said, "This is what will happen if you pay attention only to your goal (bridge) and not the roads towards it." Vipul says, "Let's go back, then," we began our journey backwards again. We walked back for five kilometres, till we reached the junction. This time, we examined the direction carefully and we realised that the bridge appears to east, but its road starts from west. The goal which was visible to us misled our direction.

I understood 'The way to it' is different from the 'The way it is seen' as.

REAL MEANING OF EDUCATION IS TOLD

"Look for ways to solve them, ask what is going wrong and the answer is your thoughts." I suddenly realised there is somebody who understood what I am going through. I look up and it is Dev's maid. I am in Kolkata to celebrate Durga Puja in my friend house and now a lady with half broken teeth, unwashed clothes, as ugly as anyone could be is speaking to me.

I smile and she, "Your thoughts are pulling powerful forces and a spirit guides you every moment. Have you heard of it?" I am least aware what she is talking. But I know spirit talks to all of us. She continues, "Yes, when you ignore them, your blessings turn evil," she goes on, "have you experienced events that were unavoidable and when you tried to avoid them, they chased you more?" I immediately answered, "Yes Bai," (Bai is the term used to address elderly women in respect)

There were many problems that had reoccurred. I had lost many, I have gained many, but I know most of them had blind spotted me. Those situations happened even after I did my best to control. Bai continues, "It is the spirit, the godly spirit. They are reminding you something very important. You should use them to evolve. Godly spirit talks to you every day. They send messages in the form a situation. The whole universe depends on these messages to live, expect humans."

I knew at once she knows the language of universe. I continued with a smile, "Yes, I have read and learnt that 'Nothing happens by coincidence, everything is interconnected' in most of the books. I hope you knew how to read." She, "Knowing how to read, is not enough. Knowing how to read the language of universe is the real essence of success. My mother taught me how to read these signs.

You have spent half of your life in concrete buildings to learn how to read. You have read thousands of books to know what I have already learnt. Our ancestors did not go to any concrete building, but they all had enough understanding, to control their destiny." She holds a broom and continues, "Everything cannot be understood in those concrete buildings. Sometimes they make your thoughts limited. The thoughts make you to ignore what you should really know: The language of universe. I can interpret your signs, I can even predict your future, everything because I follow a spirit, the spirit of the world."

I am astonished because I can know my future, I ask, "What is my future then?"

She laughs, "This is what the education does. Depend on somebody else words. I can tell you right now, but I won't, because I want you to learn on your own, the spirit will guide you, only if you are really in need of them.

The concrete building has limited your thinking ability. People think that education gives them everything, but education withdraws the basic manners of respecting everyone. Do you respect a beggar, as much as you respect a company's CEO?"

I smile,

She asks, "Tell me honestly"

I, "No, I don't."

She frowns, "This is what education does to the world. Okay why don't you respect the beggar?"

I, "Well I don't know. Maybe he begs. He could work instead."

Bai adds, "Does that mean you should not respect him, because he is not doing what you think he should do," she asks again, "okay, let us not consider a beggar, let us consider an untidy maid like me, who works for her bread. I ask the same question, 'Do you respect me as much as you respect a millionaire?'

My honest answer, "No."

She asks, "Why?"

I said, "Because you have not studied in that concrete building or you don't have enough money."

"Does that mean you should not respect me?

"Okay, tell me, can you fix this leaking tap?"

"No, I can't."

She asks, "Can you stitch a Salwar Kameez."

"No, I can't."

She, "Does this mean I know certain things, more than you?"

I agreed.

She, "Then, how is that I am not educated in my own field?

This is what your concrete buildings have taught you. To qualify everything based on their definition. They define what is education and what is not, and you agree."

I nodded, "We would have a merrier world, if there were no definitions."

Pointing at some money on the table, Bai continues, "Those mere papers will define the concept of my respect right? They have more papers, I have more happiness. Who is rich here? If you define rich as abundant wealth, then I too have some abundant wealth. The wealth of loving my mother, I take care of my health more cautiously than anybody else. Isn't love or happiness a wealth? No, not in the definition of your concrete buildings, because they do not have the skill to measure and quantify valuable possessions like these.

Everybody have their own frequency of possessing certain things. So why do we revere one possession to be higher than other, when each of them have their own important roles to play," she sips water, "I see lot of people everyday who disrespect some race, religion, job, financial status. Does that make them feel great about themselves? So if you have learnt not to respect somebody, does that make you feel educated?

Answer is people think this way - I don't want to show respect to them, because I am a great person. What is the logic here?"

I know that she is speaking something, what the world is ignorant about; learning to respect everyone. A mere certificate is not enough to be called educated. We all get disrespected for one reason or the other, because people think that disrespecting makes them a great person. I have also seen some of my friends who turn their respect off to someone with dirty shoes. Again I have the same question. How does disrespecting someone, makes them feel superior? Who is educated here? The person who wears dirty shoes and respects everyone or the person who wears clean shoes and disrespects him?

Now I try hard to understand the real meaning of education. Bai knows certain things more than me. She has the basic manners to respect everyone, she comes across. She has a great sense of connection with something bigger than us; a miraculous power. Then why does the world define such people as illiterate. The best behaviour, accompanied with pure heart, the ability to win their bread is all enough to be defined as well-educated, and that should demand respect.

"EVERYTHING ELSE IS MADE UP, BUT THE TRUTH IS LOVE" SHE QUOTES

Ma'am, "Sweets."

My teacher, "What's the occasion?"

I said, " Ma'am it's my birthday."

Teacher, "Wow, then it's a very special day," my professor continues with delight, "Birthdays are a very special day. You are his thoughtful creation. Do you know what god wants? 'Your happiness'," she points her index finger towards my chest, "All he wants is, you to be happy with his work. I know he has all the faith, that you will make the best use of his gift: Your life."

From this day on, my birthday becomes a special event for me. Every year is celebrated in its own unique manner. Some birthdays are spent in isolation; I just recline on sofa, drink an apple juice and thank god for creating me. Some years, I have pool of loved ones to celebrate my birthday. Some years, I do not receive a single birthday wish and other years, I may be flooded with birthday gifts. Some years all alone on bed, some years with family and friends and some years in solo trips. Irrespective of who is there with me, who is not, who wishes me, who doesn't, birthday is always a celebration, because I am the god's own reality.

This year, I am excited to celebrate my birthday with my boyfriend, Zoober. Zoober books a table at the most expensive restaurant for the celebration. As a customary law, I wear an expensive frock, carry a clutch from prestigious brand, combined with sophisticated silhouettes. Deep down my mind, I ignored my freedom to wear something that makes me comfortable. As Bai had said earlier, concrete buildings teaches us to wrap our brain's dirt in the most appealing attire. I know that my dirt will be least recognised, when I wear my best clothes.

We take a taxi to this restaurant at 7 p.m. We walk inside and to our surprise, we hear that the tables are not reserved for us.

Zoober, "We had booked a table three days ago."

The Guest Relation Manager, "I am really sorry sir, there was a problem in our software. Can you wait for an hour? We will get a table for you as soon as possible."

Zoober, "No I think, we will go to some other restaurant. We have other plans tonight."

Zoober googles and books a table in another good place called 'Out and box'. We walk till the middle of street to get a taxi. At 8 o'clock, the taxi driver drops us to a street, adjacent to the restaurant. We walk for five hundred meters and move inside.

The restaurant looks untidy. It lacks sufficient brightness that a human eye usually needs. We walked little more and we notice the broken stairs everywhere. The receptionist directs us to head left and as we did, we land at an eating area. This place looks least elegant. The ceilings are partially broken. It has uncomfortable wooden chairs and tables. We are disappointed. We thought of moving to another place, by then a waiter welcomes us and asks us to sit. He serves us water and politely, "I will get the menu." I reply, "Can you change our table?" He agreed. He then carefully examined different tables, checked the artificial breeze from the AC and directed us towards another table. We sat there.

Zoober, "We will have a beer from this place and go to a five star hotel." I agreed. For us, my birthday had to be celebrated in the best place and according to us, the most expensive places are the best places.

Zoober calls the waiter, "Can you get some chocolates, it's my girlfriend's birthday."
The waiter nods and with a smile and asks, "What is her name?"
Zoober "Chaitra"

"I will get a menu for local desserts and chocolates have a look at it sir." We nod our heads. As soon as he disappeared, Zoober starts searching for a better place. We start conversing about other possibilities.

Few minutes later, the waiter appears with a small cake carved on it, 'Happy Birthday Chaitra.' I am surprised. All the waiters now gather around us and say, "It's a gift from all of us sir." This is something really special. I once again got deeply connected to a gift of god:love.

Now, at no point, I start to think about my understanding about birthday celebration. 'Expensive restaurants, good clothes and money?' I question again 'Why do I believe that life's best time is spent only in expensive places.' I turn to Zoober and ask, "Why does money gauge the quality of celebration. Zoober smiled, "We were wrong. We are made to believe in world's lie once again; that the celebration is monetary value. Your birthday is special, that doesn't mean, expensive places prove that for you." he laughs

This small restaurant showed us universal essence of love. The waiters are rich here. Rich in god's definition of abundance. Their love surpassed the quality of any expensive restaurant. Most expensive restaurants do what we ask for, only for money. They might have asked us, 'Do you wish to get a cake for birthday' again with an expectation of 'Selling'. From service to food, everything revolves around 'Selling'. But there is something here, the abundance of love that filled the place.

At this point, I reshape my thoughts; money does not set a standard in quality, but a love does. I ask myself again, "Why do people set a monetary value to define the quality of their celebration. Why people show their love is greater by setting a price every time? Does spending time with elite community, following the life style set by them, paying more attention to appearance and setting a value to everything based on price, define best time?"

I think for me a broken ceiling, filled with generosity, warmth and love is more expensive. I learnt again that god gifts us something more than money, but we never realise it.

Indeed this was a special birthday. What could have been better than celebrating birthday with people who treated you more like a family.

A small move by them made a valuable move for us. It was one of the best birthday celebrations, with unknown people having family's heart.

SHE LEARNS, THE REASON BEHIND MISERY

There is this beautiful place called Wayanad in India. Mother Nature has bestowed her generosity in this place. This place has an underlying order from nature, to live in harmony. The forests, mountain, rivers all have their unique roles to be played, for harmony.

The larger mountains here display the vastness of time and space. The vast space reflects the infinity of human mind that has exceptional powers; that can change your world or destroy them; everything depends on 'what you believe is the truth.'

The fierce rain elevated our joys deep inside. The buzzing sound of wind, cool breeze from the rain, all of them lit our moods at our office Nfaktor.

My colleague Kanha called me and some of his close friends, "Let's plan a trip to Wayanad."

Neelam, another colleague continued, "Yes, we have a long weekend this week. We have to book the rooms fast, the price would surge up."

I immediately said, "I am in."

All of us agreed to take the plan ahead and booked the resorts on the following day. As a customary habit, we informed our boss Madhav about our plan and immediately, "It is really a bad idea to go there during Monsoon." Now another colleague joins the discussion, "Yeah, you should have checked the weather forecast, look it's clearly shown that it will rain," pointing at Google weather forecast.

We are taken back. Yet Kanha, "Let's go ahead. We will at least learn to handle the adverse. It's all about experience. There is no point backing out because of nature's cycle. We cannot avoid something that is natural."

On June 10, we all packed for Wayanad. We are seven in number, five of us chose to travel by car, remaining two opted to travel in a bike. It is an amazing day. The clouds are waiting to burst their joy, in the form of rain. Mother earth eagerly waits to welcome them. She knows the importance of every force of nature. The rain, keeps her children alive and so she and her favourite children, trees, are ready to embrace them. I can feel the cool breeze, pacing up to our car's speed just to make us feel their presence. The water droplets are forming on our car windows and tickling down immediately, honouring the permanent temporariness.

Now there is a buzzing sound of rain all around me. Every sound has a soul in them; soul of emotions. These souls often get connected and that becomes music. I am able to hear this pleasant music of rain. The music that has a language; the language of my emotion. The rain sings in delight,

"We are sent by the god and so are you. All of us are his magical creation.
We are all created by same force.
The force that binds us together
The force that aligns us
The force that forms us
The force that pulls us together
Everything is created by a force
Don't fight against your forces. They are clean, clear and have a purpose.
Don't fight against it, embrace it as mother earth embraces us.
We give chills, we spread cold, but we are here for a reason.
Without us there will be no life.
And so are the natural forces of your life
Every situation, carry their own essence
Don't fight against it, embrace it, Don't fight against it embrace it."

I experience a force inside me. I am getting attracted to something important. The god's version of truth. The truth that lies beneath every soul. The truth that is always manipulated-The god's version of truth.

We suffer because we are made to understand that we can change every circumstance. But no circumstance can be altered without changing our beliefs. We suffer because we feel sorry about our situations. We blame our circumstances and we wish, we could change it. We complain about everything we could think we can change. But we never give a single thought of changing ourselves. We hold our beliefs tight and we again consider that what we believe is right. Those beliefs create pain. The attempts to fit, inside the beliefs of the world create pain. Should we change our beliefs or the natural forces?

I made a review of my life altogether. The more I think about the pain I have had, the more I am realising that it was not my circumstance but my belief about how everything has to be. All the years I spent feeling sorry about my situations, in reality those situations looked miserable in the belief of the world, not in the eyes of the creator. I spent time complaining about those circumstances, but the truth lied in changing my belief. The world created certain belief about how one has to be and I followed it. It created inconvenience, I was in pain, but still I acted according to that belief. Should I can become a rebel or submissive to the world's beliefs. Everything is in my hand.

People spend all their time in worrying, but I realise that everything revolves around changing their belief about how life has to be. As I introspect, I am realising the god's version of truth, the truth that is free of beliefs. God never created any parameters for anyone's life.

I was caged, caged in the beliefs of the world. The belief that life has to be in a certain way. I know what went wrong in my life; I fought against the forces, instead of my beliefs.

"Do you need a jacket?" screamed Mike. I am distracted and I immediately open my eyes. Mike's face is turned towards Sahil and Gopal, who are driving in that fierce rain. They have tilted their heads slightly down and are carefully driving amidst the winds and heavy rain.

Sahil signs, "No" to Mike's offer. I am feeling bad for Sahil and Gopal. They are struggling hard in the rain. Sahil has to focus carefully; a slight difference in the speed can give the tyre, a chance to slide over the road. Sahil has kept his eyes and jaw tight to avoid blinking.

The visibility of the road eventually becomes dull.

Kanha, "Lets stop for Dinner."

We signed Gopal and Sahil to stop for

dinner. We now enter a restaurant that is made of yellow straws. The interiors reminded me of the historical stories, narrated in our childhood.

Sahil and Gopal wiped the dirt from their face and body. We are at the table to have delicious sambaar rice and the two boys are shivering in cold.

Kanha says, "Let's all switch our turns. This time Neelam and Mike can go on bike, every seventy kilometres we will change."

Now Neelam washes her hands, wears a thicker jacket and tries to sit on the bike. Sahil and Gopal at once screamed, "NO" with a frown. Gopal with an unaltered frown, "We are having nice time, don't try to spoil it. We don't want anyone to switch."

I am astonished by this. "How could somebody enjoy this type of situation?" and the same voice that questioned also answered, "Why can't they?" Everything lies in how you perceive your situation as. For some, worst looks adventurous and for someone else the best moments look unsatisfying.

I again refocused my thoughts on what is happening. It looked like a 'kind of struggle' for me, but it was not for them. In many situations in past, it looked like people are happy, but may be they were not. Everything revolves around how you think about the situation.

The circumstances do not make us sad, but our belief and perceptions about our circumstances controls our entire emotion.

SHE READS THE POSSIBILITIES IN SPIRITUAL WORLD

My mom and I decided to visit Chin Swee temple at Genting highlands, Malaysia. We climb the small rise and from the top, I can see the prominent statue of Buddha. I begin to walk further and I see engraved messages on the wall. From what I read about it, the possibilities in spiritual world.

Message 1
Taming Tiger Lohan- Pindola
Precious rings with magical powers
Infinitely resourceful
Vigourous and powerful
Subduing and a ferocious tiger

Pindola was a Brahmin and a general. Because he was devoted to buddhism, which forbids killing, he was ordered by the king to become a monk. He joined a monastery in the mountains where he could hear tiger howling everyday. He said that tiger was probably hungry and should be fed some vegetarian food otherwise the tiger might become a man-eater. So Pindola collected food from the monks and put it in a bucket which he left outside the monastery. The tiger did come for the food every night. After a period of time, the tiger was tamed. Thus Pindoka was referred to as the Taming Tiger Lohan.

Message 2
Long- eyebrow Lohan -Asita
Compassionate elder,
A monk who has attained enlightenment
Perspective of the infinite universe
With tacit understanding

Asita in Sanskrit means incomparably proper, or of correct proportion in spirit and physique. According to the legend Asita was born in two long eyebrows. The story was that in his previous life he was a monk who, though having tried very hard yet could not attain enlightenment even at a ripe old age, and a had only two long white eyebrows left. After his death he reincarnated as a human being again. After he was born his father was told that Shakyamuni Buddha also has two long eyebrows, therefore his son had look of the buddha in him. As a result Asita was sent away to a monastery to become a monk. Eventually attaining enlightenment.

Message 3
Scratched ear lohan- Nagasena
Leisurely and contended
Happy and knowledgeable,
Full of wit and humour,
Exuberant with interest

His sanskrit name is Nagasena, which means an army of dragons and symbolizes strong supernatural power. Nagasena was an eloquent speaker and debater. He was famous all over India for his preachings on the 'hear evil' maxim. The senses of hearing is one of the six sources through which mankind become aware of the world. Therefore a practitioner of Buddhism should avoid listening to decadent sounds and in particular other people secrets. Thus he is often portrayed as scratching his ear a gesture symbolizing the purification of the sense of hearing in the search for peace and quiet.

Message 4
Open Heart Lohan Gobaka
Open the heart and there is buddha
Each displaying his powers
The two should not compete

For Buddha's power of bondaries

Gobaka was a prince of a minor kingdom in India. When he was made crown prince, his younger brother started a rebellion. But Gobaka assured his brother that he wanted to refuse the kingdom and become a monk because he only had buddha in his heart. As a proof, he exposed his chest and there indeed was a Buddha in his heart. The younger brother then believed him and stopped the rebellion. Gobaka become a monk it is believed that Gobaka was the monk Shan Wu Wel.who arrived at Chang'an during the Tang Dynasty 710 A.D.Gobaka literally means 'man of heart' weak physically but strong of spirit.

Message 5
Laughing Lion Lohan-vajra putra
Playful and free of inhibitions
The lion cub leaps with joy
Easily alternating tension with relaxation
Rejoicing with a living things

Vajra Putra literally means 'man of cats' . He was a lion hunter before he was converted to Buddhism. After he had attained enlightenment, a little lion came playfully to his side. The animal seemed to be grateful to him for giving up the life of killing lions, thus sparing its parents and brothers. Since then Vajra Putra and a little lion have become inseparable. The lion, with its earth-shaking roar, symbolizes the invincible might of Buddhism. Therefore, it is very common to find a pair of lions standing guard at the front gate of a buddhist temple or monastery in China.

UNDERSTANDS THE GOD'S REALITY

'It would be great if I do some Volunteering, while I am here," said Lisa.

I, "I am interested too, how can we do this?"

Lisa, "Teach English. It will be great to work with children."

I said, "I want to join, but when should we do it".

Lisa, "Anytime, when we are free, service to humanity does not need time. One of my acquaintances, study at Ghounzhou, Institute of Foreign studies. May be she can help us." We take a bus from Yongtai and go to Guangdong University of Foreign Studies. We meet Anna.

"Hi we would like to know more about China's culture, is there any kind of volunteering that gets us know more about China?"

Anna, "Well, I will not ask you any questions, because at least you are making an effort to be part of this, during your free time," gives us the form to fill and continues, "I know an opportunity, it works this way. You will teach English and we give you different home stays with Chinese local families."

I, "That sounds interesting." Anna continues, "You will know more about their life, Chinese food and traditions and so on." We filled the form and then walked back to our workplace.

The following week, we visit many families and we are surprised to know that these families are willing to give us the luxurious rooms and delicious meal; all of them, free of cost. Now, when the entire universe whirl around to get maximum benefits from their actions, how could these people give us stay and meal for six to eight long weeks with no financial expectations. Many people are embracing the idea of providing a comfort stay to backpackers, but it does include some little fees.

Expectations act as a substitute to human actions. These set of expectations actually change the outlook of our life. We want to have some kind of degree with an expectation of getting job or satisfying our prestige. We adopt kindness, but deep inside, it is only with an expectation of getting blessed by god or get same returns from those people. Most of us, want to be a good human, because our religious scriptures teaches us to be. In fact most of the religious scriptures say if you want to be close to god, be kind. So one knows that he gets what he wants, when he is close to god. So again where does the real intention lies in?

Two other Chinese Volunteers accompany me to show my home stay. We take a bus to Renhe. Ferry briefs me "You will stay with a Chinese couple. A small family of two: Mandy and her husband Ron. The lady is interested to see you. She likes Indians. She wants to learn English from you. She will be very happy to see you." I am very happy, to hear that she will be happy to see me. After all, I feel obliged to stay with them for no financial benefit.

The bus stopped at Renhe and we walked for hundred meters. We wait at the lobby of the apartment and we get a message, "Come to sixth floor." I am curious, to see Mandy, her husband and their heart to humanity.

Mandy, opens the door, and I see two dogs behind her. Now I am very scared of dogs, how can I stay in this house? Mandy sensed my fear and puts them in balcony. With relief I enter the house. The drawing room is very spacious, with a Chinese lantern placed at the centre. The main wall is covered with the huge poster of one of the great saints of India and I immediately, "God believers always do good to people."

Mandy, Ferry and Mint showed me my room. The interiors have delicate Chinese designs.

The Statues of Buddha and Indian saints are placed near the entrance. On the right side of the room stands a contemporary pillar, holding Chinese lanterns. The bed is placed towards south east of the room, which can skilfully receive first glimpses of sun, at dawn. The cupboards are small and clean and each cupboard has a huge space, symbolising the vast space we hold within ourselves. While I was appreciating the beauty of my room, Mandy invited us to dining room for dinner. The dining room was the expansion of the kitchen. Altogether the interiors were designed to ensure that the prayer and eating rooms should have maximum space.

Mandy serves dumpling on my plate and asks, "Can you teach me yoga?"

I feel happy now and I say, "Yes."

"That's great," she says, while adding red curry on my plate. We all now take a position to start the prayer before our dinner.

Mandy asks me to recite and signed rest others to chant after me

I recite ,

Om Asatoma, Sadga Maya (Lead us from the unreal to the real)

Tamasoma, Jyotirgamaya (Lead us from darkness to light)

Mruthyoma Amrutam gamaya (Lead us from death

to immortality)

Om Shanti, Shanti, Shantihi (Aum peace, peace, peace)

We now start to hog the delicious Chinese-Korean dinner cooked by Mandy's husband. Mandy, "I want to learn English, that's why I thought of staying with a foreigner who could teach me English," I felt really nice because I can be of some use to her in return of food and shelter. She then speaks about the preaching of her spiritual leader and said, "*Anna Data Sukino Bhava,*" (serving food to people can bring you good fortune). Mandy, "So, I invite people for food." The conversation goes well and I go to sleep.

*

Mandy knocks my door, "Breakfast ready, I have prepared Rice Porridge and Walnut Milkshake for you."

I said, "That's really nice of you. Thank you so much."

We sat on the chair and Mandy said "Teach me yoga."

I agreed.

We started with Ardhachakrasana and she found it tough. I taught her two more Asanas and she was not able to do. Mandy gets disappointed.

I, "It's your first day. It takes time to be flexible."

She replies, "I don't think yoga suits me, teach me English from tomorrow."

I agreed. Mandy then goes to meditation and I sleep for a while.

Mandy spends two hours in meditation every day, but to my surprise, I have never seen her happy. She is kind; she is doing good service to humanity, why is god not bestowing her with what she wants? Why her only misery of not having a child, cannot be resolved, despite being kind and a god believer?

Days pass and I start becoming a common person in the house. I start going out for breakfast, lunch and dinner because Mandy becomes busy. Though fear of the dogs always troubled me, they spent most of the time in the balcony. Few more days pass, Mandy stops talking to me. Things become uncomfortable between us. 'Why is she upset with me? Something wrong I did to her?'

A week later, I called Anna and told her to find me another home stay and gives her the reason, 'I am scared of dogs.' To my surprise Anna tells me, "Yes, I am doing it because Mandy has asked me to look out a new home stay for you. Again I asked myself, 'What made her so upset with me? I failed to teach English well or Yoga?'

Following week, Anna takes me to a new home stay, now a question arises, 'How do I meet their expectations? What if I am asked to go?'

Anna and my few friends drop me to my new home stay. This is a three member family; with a couple and their little child. The family is an atheist family. The home stay man, John welcomes us, offers us Chinese tea and takes us around the house to show me shops and restaurants. I say good bye to my friends and go inside the house. John, "Come, I will show you, your room."

The room looks like a small doll house with many teddies and Lego toys. I feel light like a baby with this beauty and I move around. I see a thin tapestry and I open. The beautiful green mountain offers me a generous smile from far.

John asks, "Are you happy with the room?"

I said, "Yes, very much."

"Let's go to the kitchen," he takes me to kitchen, shows me the fridge and with a smile, "you can have anything and everything from the fridge,' he points at Chinese cooker and says, "You can boil eggs here for breakfast."

Everything starts progressing in a satisfactory manner, while I waited for some expectations. But nothing as such happened. John and his wife prepared dinner for me every day, took me out during weekends, treated me in different restaurants, so that I can get flavour of China. One night John knocked my door, "We are feeling cold, I thought you must be too, take this double quilt blankets, it keeps you warm."

They were very happy in life. Every dinner John and his wife shared their happy stories with the kid. They were going to cultural trips every month and their life was a real inspiration for me.
This day, I realise one thing and I write in my diary. A realisation about god and blessings. It is not always about belief in god that gives us happiness, it is sometimes about being happy with what we have.

There was a huge difference between John and Mandy, it was not about Kindness, but with the way they understood their lives. Mandy meditated for two hours a day, followed ideals of great saints, believed in god, involves in charity, and does everything and anything to get what she wants. But she is not happy. All her attempts go in vain for one reason; she sets rules to become happy. She is taught, 'Do good to others, god will bestow you with what you want.' So every time Mandy makes this attempt, she is expecting something good from god. When her expectations are not being met, she ends up getting disappointed.

I begin to remember my master's words:
*"How can one spread kindness, when they are not
kind to themselves?*
*How can one spread happiness, when they are not
happy with themselves?*
*How can one love others, when they cannot love
themselves?"*
When she is harming herself with disappointments, sadness, depressions, how can she try to spread something opposite to what she is going through.

She never spent time nurturing herself with kindness.
Forgive herself, when things went wrong.
Give herself, a second chance, whenever she failed
Keeping faith in her

That's why she expected great things in life, in return for her kindness. She never experienced happiness in charities or humanity services. She was in it, expecting god's favour.

But on other hand, John spreads kindness with no expectations. He does it, because he loves to do it. He does not believe in god and so he never set rules, according to our assumptions about god. He has learnt to find happiness in himself, which manifests itself to the miraculous energy and he gets what he wants.

I again remember my master's words, "Energy surrounds all of us. Universe returns you with those things, you give more attention to. You get what you want, when you have good energy around you and that is called god."

This whole experience made me understand one thing. A man gets into next level of spirituality of helping others, when he experiences kindness, empathy and love for himself. You spread what you have. You get back what you spread.

I got a better understanding of concept of Aham Brahmasi from Brihadaranyaka Upanishad in Hinduism. The great saint Adi Shankara explains Aham Brahmasmi; meaning supreme god is in you.

To see god, one has to be god. You know god, when you are god. You will know happiness, when you have happiness. You get what you want, when you know what you have. Be your own love, your own happiness, your own kindness.

You are brahma's(god) supreme reality. You understand infinite energy of possibilities, when you see god in you and your life.

SHE UNDERSTANDS THE POWER OF DIVINE ENERGY

My mom once said, "It's not always GPS, talk to people, they guide you." I have realised that it's better to connect to people than technology.

Driven by the idea to connect to more people and less technology, I have declined the use of GPS for directions. And to my honour, I have always received enough help to get directions, irrespective of type of country or race. I believe that when you connect to somebody, you are always connected to them by heart. You start to develop a spiritual connect with them because you are helped by them and they are thanked by you.

I am in Beijing lu, China buying some accessories. I finished my shopping and headed to go home. I missed my way. I turn towards a lady who is around twenty meters away from me,

"Hi, can you talk in English?"

The lady with a charming smile, "Yes very much. How can I help you?"

I ask, "Can you tell me, where is the nearest metro station?" The lady, "Little far, you have to walk around one kilometre. Where do want to go?"

I , "To Suyuan."

The lady, "I am going to Xiangang. The stop before yours. I will come with you." We walk together and the lady asks me my reason to be in China. I explain. She continues, "I do freelancing; education projects for children." I, "That's amazing. You might be aware of the future already," with laughter.

The lady continued, "Yes. You see, divine energy surrounds all of us. It creates a set of possibilities each day, to reach our destiny; only if we follow them. She pauses for a second and continues, "But our youth have forgotten this; to follow their path of divinity. Each one of us, reach our path in a different way. Your path isn't same as mine or my path isn't same as yours. Based on that, we face different situations and each of these situations has its own way of learning. There is a unique ability in each one of us to interpret this learning, which makes or break our destiny.

Now that I see everyone walk the path that does not belong to them. They follow either because world thinks it right or they don't understand their road and the most dangerous thing is walking the roads too fast." I agreed, "It is a fast moving life with slow realisation. Children spend their adolescence in rush and then regret about the things they did not do. Every age has its own joy of living, but we are adhering to the fast success, fast wealth and so we are losing the joy associated with every age."

I nodded, she points at some children on other side of the pavement, "The concept of achieving everything being young, makes the life fruitless, thereafter. Neither you experience the taste of youth nor you experience the art of living in old age.

The divine energy creates paths and their dimension of time. Everything will happen, only when the time lets you. Before that you will walk the road to preparation. You will get what you want, only when you are prepared enough to make the best use of this road. The road to preparation, prepares you to wisdom," she adds, "I think you are in the sphere of evolution. It's the time for you to understand, what you are going through."

"All these are running above my head."

She laughs, "It is not running over, the spirit is making you to re-collect the secrets, but you are ignoring," she continues, "A Buddhist monk once visits a small town in Chengdu province. On his arrival, he finds many people gathered there to welcome him. The monk closely observes the crowd and he finds a spirit in a man's eyes; Spirit to evolute.

The monk asks the man to take him to his house. The man becomes very happy and invites him for lunch. The following day, monk visits the man's house.

The house has partially broken roof. The walls of the drawing room are falling apart. On entering the backyard, there was one cow in the shed. The monk asks the man 'What is this for?' The man replies, 'This cow is our only treasure. I sell its milk everyday and feed my four children and wife. I sell its dung as a fertilizer which helps me to pay my children's school fees. Our half of the meal is from this cow.'

The monk smiles and asks the man to give that cow to him. The poor man becomes angry by monk's demand. He clarifies that the cow is the only treasure and their life will become miserable. Still the monk demands the cow. The poor man gives the cow, with great pain. The monk leaves the place.

The poor man spends his days crying over the cow. He wished monk should not have come to his house.

Years pass, the monk visits the poor man's house again. Rather than finding the same house, the monk finds a big house. On entering the bungalow, he sees a hive of activities; the tradesmen are doing some trade in the house. There is a huge pile of grains, placed to the east of the room. The monk asks for the poor man but to his surprise no one knows what he is talking about.

When he is about to leave, the poor man appears from the room. He invites the monk and thanks him. The monk asks, 'How come you have become so wealthy?'

Man says, 'I found my treasure.'

The monk smiles, 'What was treasure?'

The man replies, 'The treasure is pain,' he continues with gratitude, 'You took away my only treasure, a cow. We spent days in starvation. We hated you. My wife and I decided to kill ourselves. We did not know what to do.

One day, my wife suggested that we shall try sowing some grains in our backyard. We cleaned the shed and we sowed some seeds. In few days, we got our first set of green peas. We put some more of it and then in three months we were left with three big bags of green peas. My wife then used the other barren lands in our backyard to sow some berry seeds. In less than six months we had twelve bags of berries. We got to know that the soil is fertile. We tried all other crops, we failed, we reaped as well.

After some days, instead of one, we bought three cows. We got double of what we were getting. Some more days passed we bought hens. Now we have everything what we wanted.'

He touches the feet of the monk, 'If you had not given us the pain, we would not have known the value behind the pain. The cow was not our source of treasure, but a block of treasure.'

The monk smiles, 'Master appears when the student is ready. Sometimes all you have to do is take risks. When you cannot do that, the divine energy takes away your most important things.'

'Dreams come true. You get everything, only when you are ready to accept them with fullness. When I saw you, I knew that you were ready. You just had to know the pain, to rebuild your destiny.' The lady continues, "Master appears when the student is ready. The master comes in the form of situations. It is called evolution."

In a slow motion, my life became a giant universe. I inspected every particle of divine energy and started to interpret its presence. My life is in perfect sphere of evolution. The spirit in me is guiding me right. Everything is beginning to make sense to me.

The divine grace is showing me my way. My way to move to the next level of spiritual dimension. I am achieving that peace. 'Everything starts from the way you interpret your situations,' said a divine voice. I looked at the lady and there is a charm and I realised that we are bound by a force. The force that touches all of us, when we are ready.

The sensation is striking my flesh and soul. I am going through a pleasure. The worldly joy is manifested in me freely, moving inside.

I allowed myself to be let by this woman. She takes me to the nearest monastery.

1 YEAR, 4 SEASONS

"I had often fallen down, only to know where I should be careful," I told her. I continued what I had learnt all these days, "I know that everything is predestined, but I can change my destiny however I want with my magical forces. I want to know more about these forces." The lady smiles, "The secret loses its value, if everything is revealed. I can only take you to certain direction and the rest, the divine energy guides you, when you are ready."

"There is a connection between your thoughts and the forces that binds all of us in the world," she said,

"I know this; it's the law of attraction."

She, "Tell me what do you know, I can then help you."

I continued, "The seasons are the first set of universal forces that told me something important. I understood three important things. The first principal: You cannot change what is written, but everything will change, when the time permits. The second one: You cannot escape any season, you have to experience every season and understand its importance. The third one: Nothing lasts forever. There is a comfort in knowing that seasons change and everything will and shall change."

I saw that the lady's eyes, lit up like a candle in my dark room, "You are in the perfect sphere to understand every principal, set by divine energy. You see, universe reveals something important. Everyone can contemplate the beauty of this in their own way. Everything is based on how they interpret their signs. The first principal is in learning how you combine the laws of nature with your own life.

The divine energy guides you at three crucial moments. First is when you are in pain, second is when your orbits begin to change and the third is when your thoughts emit a higher frequencies. Everything starts in the form of a pain. It's the indication, something has to change."

I asked, "Then what is the solution for the pain?" She replied, "Imagining the best, can determine your future."

I said, "It's the law of attraction."

She replies, "Exactly"

She smiled, "As I said there is a beauty in everything. When you see the beauty, things start to make sense."

My mind started working, to connect my dots from what I had experienced with pine trees, the trekking experiences, the farmhouse owner, I recollected every single experience and there is miraculous power in all of them. I continued, "Everything should change. Our thoughts should change, our perception should change and our situations will change, that is what the first universal force; seasons, teaches us."

She said, "You are right. You should be flexible just like the pine trees," as though she knew what was in my mind.

I said, "I want to say one more thing I had been to trekking and I learnt how to notice every path I walk."

She, "Never forget those roads, once you think you are successful, same roads are required to accomplish something else."

She continued, "I think you are aware of your first spiritual dimension. Practice your learning every day."

"Can you teach me, how to move to next sphere of evolution?"

She smiled, "The spirit always guides you. Pay attention to its signs," she continued with a smile again "Anyways I will tell you another code. It's Colour and Aura. Imagine them inside and outside you. They will bring strong current to your forces."

"I did not understand"

She, "You will not, because you have not yet practised your learning seriously. There is a language in every element of earth and there is a vibration in every part of earth. We are all bound by the forces of these vibrations. Know that, love can control those vibrations." She looks around and thinks for a while, "The creator applies the same of laws of nature for us as well; Law of evolution.

God created everything for purpose and he has given us all the freedom to control our lives, change our destiny, if we want to. EVERYTHING LIES IN IMAGINING THE BEST."

Now I look at what the world taught me all these years. The world preached lies. Somebody in the past said, 'Money brings happiness.' The world designed whole course around it. Somebody said, 'Achieving something young is pleasant, everybody followed. Somebody said success means more money and everybody followed. Somebody said failure is evil, everybody followed.

She said, "These lies were created by people who couldn't control the forces of universe. The forces of divinity were beyond their comprehension. So they created something that is easily understood. They called this reality and everyone followed. What everybody understood were called real, the rest were defined as unreal. Then, the evil was born. Our vibrational frequencies reduced. Ultimately world lost the power to miracles."

"You are right." The sun now begins to sink down the horizon. The flames of this fireball that emitted a heat wave from the distance of 149.6 million kilometres, finally makes a soft touch on me with accurate warmth. The wind is moving at pleasant speed of five miles per hour. These forces are reminding me that there is a way to deal with them.

The divine energy is connecting me to these forces. I am in a magical world. Life is a miracle. I opened my eyes; I am born again with a true reality.

1 YEAR 4 SEASONS